ANN RICHARDS

"A WOMAN'S PLACE IS IN THE DOME"

ANN RICHARDS
"A WOMAN'S PLACE IS IN THE DOME"

April D. Stumpff

Illustrated by Patrick Messersmith

State House Press

Buffalo Gap, Texas

Library of Congress Cataloging-in-Publication Data

Stumpff, April D.
    Ann Richards : "a woman's place is in the dome" / April D. Stumpff; illustrated by
Patrick Messersmith.
        p. cm.—(Stars of Texas series)
    Includes bibliographical references and index.
    ISBN-13: 978-1-933337-12-8 (hardcover: alk. paper)
    ISBN-10: 1-933337-12-5 (hardcover: alk. paper)
1. Richards, Ann, 1933-2006—Juvenile literature. 2. Women governors—Texas—
Biography—Juvenile literature. 3. Governors—Texas—Biography—Juvenile literature.
4. Texas—Politics and government—1951—Juvenile literature. I. Messersmith, Patrick.
II. Title.

 F391.4.R53S78 2008
976.4'063092–dc22
[B]

2008004995

State House Press
P.O Box 818
Buffalo Gap, TX 79508
(325) 572-3974
www.mcwhiney.org/press

Distributed by Texas A&M University Press Consortium
(800) 826-8911
www.tamu.edu/upress

Printed in the United States of America

ISBN-13: 978-1-933337-12-8
ISBN-10: 1-933337-12-5

Book designed by Rosenbohm Graphic Design

The Stars of Texas Series

Other books in this series include:
Henrietta King: Rancher and Philanthropist
Mirabeau B. Lamar: Second President of Texas
Miriam "Ma" Ferguson: First Woman Governor of Texas
Martín de León: Tejano Empresario
Audie Murphy: War Hero and Movie Star

Free workbooks available on-line at
www.mcwhiney.org/press

To Josh for always supporting and encouraging me and Johnathan who is a joy and inspiration in my life. The two of you have helped me fulfill my dreams and create new ones along the way.

CONTENTS

INTRODUCTION

*****

One of the greatest governors in Texas was just as well known for her straight-talking politics as she was for her big, white hair and sassy attitude. When Ann Richards was born, the idea of her being governor one day was nearly unthinkable. She was raised in a time when women grew up to be wives and mothers, not politicians. She broke out of that mold and determined her own fate. Ann Richards would be a wife, a mother, and a governor of the State of Texas. Not only would she accomplish all of those things in her lifetime, but she would do it with wit and humor that would endear her to the people of Texas and the nation.

One motto heard often during the Great Depression to describe how many Americans survived on less than they had previously was, "use it up, wear it out, make it do, or do without."

Ann grew up during the Great Depression. This was an era where almost 25% of workers in America did not have jobs. Across the country, families were poor and had nothing to eat and nowhere to live. Even if people did have jobs, like Ann's father, they were sometimes forced to take a cut in pay. At home, women had to find ways to save money. In Ann's home, her mother made all the clothes and much of their food was grown in the garden. Ann was raised in this frugal lifestyle and did not know anything different until she was older and the Depression had ended.

When Ann was in college she married a man named David Richards. They had four children together named Cecile, Dan, Clark, and Ellen. While Ann was having children and keeping house, she also became active in

On her 60th birthday, Ann Richards passed the test to get her motorcycle driver license.

politics. Eventually she was elected Travis County commissioner and then State Treasurer. What she remains best known for is her time as Texas governor.

Ann Richards made the government of Texas more representative of its citizens by appointing women and minorities to positions in public office. Her lasting legacy is one of equality and inclusion. While serving as governor, Ann supported environmental causes. She fought for women's rights. She worked to improve education and funding for the schools. Ann Richards spent her time and energy making Texas a better place for all people.

Chapter 1

CHILDHOOD IN LAKEVIEW

✳✳✳✳✳

No one could imagine the little girl born on September 1, 1933, would grow up to become a motorcycle-riding, big-haired Texas governor. Dorothy Ann Willis began her life as the cherished, only child of Iona and Cecil Willis. She was born in Lakeview, Texas, a small town outside of Waco. Her parents' humble origins helped to instill the core values of hard work, integrity, and equality in Ann. These principles would serve her well throughout her life as wife, mother, and politician.

Bugtussle, Texas, was so small a town it could not be found on maps, but it existed about three miles south of Lorena. That is where Cecil Willis was born to a simple life. He grew up to be a smart, out-going man of character who easily made people laugh. Cecil dropped out of school during the tenth grade and began working at Southwestern Drug Company to help support his siblings. Due to his superior work ethic, Cecil rose quickly in the company. He eventually began to work as a salesman, where he developed relationships and trust with customers throughout his region.

Iona was adventurous for a woman in early 1900s Texas. She moved from the town of Hogjaw in Cherokee County to Waco and found a job at the Rosenberg Dry Goods Company. Shortly after relocating, Iona met Cecil on a blind date arranged by friends. Cecil was a pleasant and fun-loving young man. Iona was a sensible and frugal lady. Their opposite personalities attracted them to each other, and after two years of courtship, the couple married.

Ann grew up during the Great Depression and was as much a product of the times as of her parents' personalities. Cecil and Iona

managed their money carefully, purchasing necessities only when required, although they did consider piano and public speaking lessons a must for their daughter. The family grew their own food in a large garden. Often meals consisted of the chickens and ducks raised in their home. Iona made nearly all of Ann's clothing, as a means of saving money.

Ann learned to be responsible at an early age. She had many chores around the house. One of the more memorable chores was cleaning the leaves of an ivy plant growing on the porch. Each leaf had to shine or Ann would have to start all over again until the job was done right. There were also the more typical duties of scrubbing pots and pans, helping with meals, tending to the garden and animals, or anything else her mother needed help with.

Iona would not settle for a job poorly completed. This way of thinking stayed with Ann throughout her life.

Cecil greatly influenced his daughter's character as well. Ann went fishing and hunting with Cecil and participated in other activities that were more suited to boys at the time. One of the greatest gifts that Cecil passed on to Ann was the ability to captivate an audience with his tales. Ann fondly recalled the hours she spent listening to her father tell stories. It became obvious in her later role as a politician that she was just as enthralling a speaker as her father.

Cecil also modeled noble behavior by standing up for the rights of a teacher who was pregnant. Some members of the Lakeview School Board felt the educator should not continue teaching once her pregnancy began showing. The teacher's husband was in the army, and the family needed the extra income. As a member of the school board, Cecil successfully fought against this injustice and helped the teacher keep her job.

Ann's childhood was not just about learning lessons, work, and obligations. She also enjoyed playing with her friends. Some of Ann's childhood memories included throwing chinaberries at one another, reading *Wonder Woman* comics, riding bicycles, and climbing trees.

✳✳✳

A MOVE TO CALIFORNIA

Unfortunately Ann's childhood was interrupted by the war in Europe. World War II began for the United States with the bombing of Pearl Harbor on December 7, 1941. The war even reached the little town of Lakeview. Talk soon turned to the Nazis and the Japanese, of friends and neighbors joining the United States military, and of what the war meant to the people left at home. People participated in the war effort in any way they could manage. Gas and sugar were hard to come by and had to be rationed.

The war directly affected the Willis family when Cecil was drafted into the Navy in 1944. Ann's family was not overly affectionate, but she vividly remembered the hugs and tears before her father left to go to his new duty station in California. Iona and Ann stayed behind in Lakeview, but Iona had to work part time at Southwestern Drug because Cecil's military pay was not enough to support the family. The Willis family had its share of struggles during Cecil's absence. From these trying times, Ann learned a valuable lesson: women were capable of being self-sufficient and independent.

After a few months of separation, Iona decided the family should be reunited in California. She slaughtered the remaining chickens and picked what she could from the garden. She canned all of the food to eat during the

Chinaberries are poisonous to humans.

The government stopped drafting men with children a few weeks after Cecil was inducted. Since Cecil was already in the military, he had to continue his service.

trip to San Diego, because she was always practical and prepared. California would have a great influence on molding Ann's adult views on minorities, integration, and discrimination.

San Diego had a different culture than Central Texas. It opened a new world to Ann. She visited Balboa Park and the zoo, which held animals she had never seen before. Huge palm trees and exotic flowers grew in the coastal climate. Even simple things like dinner were approached differently. Food did not come from the back garden. Instead, everything was purchased from the grocery store. School was no longer a short walk away. Ann had to travel a block to the bus stop. On the bus she traveled into the city where she then caught a trolley the rest of the way to Theodore Roosevelt Junior High.

School created more unique memories for Ann. Texas, at the time, remained a strongly segregated state. Ann's world, until moving to San Diego, was made up almost entirely of white people. San Diego's Theodore Roosevelt Junior High was a melting pot of nationalities that exposed Ann to a variety of different backgrounds. She interacted with African-Americans, Hispanics, Asians, Italians, and many other nationalities. The smart little girl quickly realized that all children were alike, regardless of race. This simple, yet thoughtful, observation guaranteed Ann would never participate in or tolerate racial prejudice.

✳✳✳

RETURN TO TEXAS

World War II ended in 1945, and Cecil was discharged from the Navy. Although San Diego left a lasting impression on Ann, the family happily and eagerly moved back to Texas. Cecil went back to work for Southwestern Drug, and Iona set up the home in Lakeview again. Life for the Willis family returned to normal. After a couple of years, Cecil and Iona decided to move to Waco to guarantee a better education for Ann.

Enrolled at Waco High, Ann quickly established herself as a likable, funny, and smart student. She excelled in her debate class for her logical arguments and quick-thinking under pressure. Ann enjoyed working with and competing against other intelligent and capable students. She traveled with the debate team and even won the Texas Interscholastic League Double-A championship in her senior year. Winning the championship was a great accomplishment, since Double-A was the largest school classification at the time.

Attending school in Waco taught Ann lessons outside the classroom as well, one of them being the differences in social status. Everyone in Lakeview was more or less of the same status, in Waco,

Ann realized her family was not very well off compared to some of the other students. This did not particularly bother Ann or her parents, but it was another observation Ann made of what society was like beyond the confines of a small town.

Just like now, dating occupied the thoughts of most teenagers, and Ann was no exception. She had her first date at fourteen. While standing in line for punch at a dance, she became so nervous that she threw up on the girl ahead of her. She had boyfriends throughout high school, but no serious boyfriend until her senior year when she was introduced to David Richards.

Ann recalled David as being handsome, funny, and well-liked by his peers. Iona was happy with the match, because David had good manners, dressed well, and came

San Diego is the place where Ann first ate a doughnut.

When Ann was in high school, the legal drinking age was eighteen. The age limit changed to twenty-one in 1984.

from an important family in Waco. Eleanor, David's mother, was also pleased by the relationship. She saw Ann as an intelligent, out-going young lady who was able to develop her own opinions.

The young couple spent a great deal of time together during their senior year. Prom night with David was when Ann had her first drink of alcohol. They began to frequent a local roadhouse to drink beer with friends. Drinking alcohol would cause Ann a lot of trouble later in life. But at the time, Ann was a fairly typical young woman, graduating from high school and preparing to attend college.

Chapter 2

THE COLLEGE YEARS

✳✳✳✳✳

College is an exciting time for young people. It is a time of opportunities, filled with promises of a better future. After graduating from high school, Ann had several colleges interested in recruiting her, including Southern Methodist University, the University of Texas, and Baylor University, all of which offered her scholarships. Ann liked the idea of attending school in a new place away from home. However, Iona felt the family could save money if Ann lived at home and attended Baylor University in Waco, Texas.

Ann also thought of David Richards while choosing a college. Ann and David's romance was becoming more and more serious.

Eleanor, David's mother, thought the couple could use some distance from each other since they were still so young. David was sent to a college prep school named Andover on the east coast. Ann decided to attend Baylor and continue living at home.

Baylor University was established in 1845. The University was started by Robert Emmett Bledsoe Baylor, a former soldier, Baptist preacher, and judge in the Republic of Texas. The university's classes were based on an equal mix of worldly and religious education, but the school was best known for its spiritual curriculum. Chapel service was mandatory on a daily basis, religion courses were encouraged, and girls were not allowed to wear pants or shorts on campus.

In 1950, when Ann started at Baylor, academics were not the only things to worry about. Young men were still liable to be drafted into the military if they failed out of college. The possibility of being sent to fight in Korea made good students out of many of the young men

~1950

at the time. The families of many students, Ann's being one of them, worked hard to save money and send their children to college; so they could do things their parents were not able to do. These students knew they had to work hard and did not want to waste that chance. Ann had learned to work hard from watching her parents.

One of the requirements for freshmen on scholarship was to take an advanced course in debate. The class, taught by Professor Glenn Capp, was an enjoyable challenge for the students. It encouraged students to learn how best to present an argument during a debate from both sides of an issue.

Ann excelled in public speaking and earned recognition with her debate partner Shirley Frank. The team from Baylor traveled all over the states of Texas and

Robert Emmett Bledsoe Baylor, whom Baylor University is named after, helped write the Texas Constitution.

Louisiana to compete in and often win tournaments. Ann and Shirley beat a men's team at Texas A&M University in March 1952, but it was the men's team that got an invitation to debate at West Point. Ann felt this was wrong, since that team was actually the losing team. She told this to Professor Capp. Glenn Capp agreed with Ann, but could not send her team to West Point. He did, however, send them to the Southern Speech Communication Association tournament in Jackson, Mississippi, where the girls received recognition for their outstanding skills. Professor Capp and the knowledge he imparted to Ann were a very important influence in her life.

David Richards was still a part of Ann's life during this exciting time. Returning home for Christmas his fresh-

The United States Military Academy at West Point only taught male students until 1976.

David scratched himself on a rusty nail during his bachelor party and the tetanus shot caused him to swell up for his wedding day.

man year, David refused to go back east again. Eleanor Richards allowed her son to remain in Texas for his college education, but only if he attended the University of Texas in Austin. David agreed to this because he would be close enough to drive home to Waco on the weekends and see Ann.

Ann and David each joined social groups on their campuses, but they had very different experiences. Ann came to learn that membership to her sorority was based more on background and what your family did for a living than on the type of person you were. Because of this, Ann chose not to be a part of the sorority any more. David, on the other hand, greatly enjoyed fraternity life focusing on parties and socializing.

***

MARRIED LIFE

After a year and a half in Austin, David decided he did not want to be away from Ann any more and transferred to Baylor. Ann chose to give up the debate team since the constant practice, preparations, and tournaments took her away from David. The young couple now spent as much time together as possible, often socializing and talking politics with friends and family. Ann and David decided it was time to get married and chose May 30, 1953, as their wedding date. It was the end of their junior year, Ann was nineteen, David was twenty, and they were very much in love.

The couple set up their new apartment and continued to attend college. As was expected of women in the 1950s, Ann cooked, cleaned, and even worked part-time in a dress shop to help with living expenses. At the end of the school year, Ann graduated with a degree in speech and political science. David earned his degree in history. They decided the next step after graduation was to move to Austin where David could study law and Ann could get her teaching credentials.

Upon earning her teaching certificate from the University of Texas, Ann began working at Fulmore Junior High School instructing eighth graders in social studies. She greatly enjoyed teaching, although she said it was the hardest work she had ever done. The challenge to get students interested in the subject and remember what they have learned remains an obstacle to teachers even today.

While Ann taught school, David studied law, but they always found time to go to Scholz Beer Garden. Students, politicians, lawyers, and regular customers chose this as the spot to meet and talk about politics. It was here that the Richardses started meeting people and getting involved in politics. David became active in the University of Texas

Young Democrats, even being elected their President. David did not know how to organize and conduct a meeting, so Ann was elected Parliamentarian because of her knowledge. Ann and David would remain in politics, in some form, for many years to come.

David graduated from law school and began working at a Dallas firm that focused on labor law. Ann was pregnant with their first child and went back to Waco to have the baby where Iona and Eleanor could help. David worked hard at being a lawyer, and Ann worked hard at becoming a mother.

A daughter, Cecile, was born on July, 15, 1957. The little girl was named after Ann's father, Cecil Willis. Six weeks later, the new mother and daughter moved to Dallas to be with David and start their new life as a family. Ann

A Parliamentarian keeps order during debates or meetings.

Before integration, black students had to attend separate schools from white students. Brown v. Board of Education of Topeka was the U.S. Supreme Court case that overturned segregation.

was happy in the role of homemaker. She cooked, cleaned, and made clothes for Cecile while David worked. She soon found that she could not stay out of politics. Ann helped by doing things like stuffing envelopes and putting up yard signs.

Being liberal in Texas was not common in those days, but Ann's political views were shaped by many of the events she perceived as unfair at the time. One example was that Texas still had not integrated its schools, even after the United States Supreme Court ruling that said it needed to be done. Ann was a strong supporter of minority rights and was actively involved in the civil rights movement.

While Ann was pregnant with their second child, Dan, David bought a house in Dallas for their growing family. David continued to participate in local politics, political campaigns, and the Young Democrats. When John F. Kennedy was elected to the Presidency in 1960, David wanted to be involved in politics at the national level. He became an attorney at the Civil Rights Commission in Washington, D.C. The Richards family packed their belongings and moved to the nation's capital. They only stayed for one year and then moved back to Dallas where they felt more useful.

Upon their return to Dallas, the Richards family welcomed their third child, Clark, in 1962. Even with three small children, Ann was not one to sit idly on the sidelines. She and several of her friends founded the North Dallas Democratic Women, an organization that focused on women being involved in politics as more than envelope stuffers. The women helped to develop campaign plans, contact voters, and track progressive Democrats on three-by-five inch index cards, which were stored in Ann's house.

Although Ann was the leader of these political and social gatherings, her family always came first. She still planned birthday parties, entertained friends, and did all the things expected of a wife and mother. In 1963, the Richards family was completed with the birth of a daughter, Ellen.

For the next few years, the Richards family continued their nonstop social life, hosting parties and discussing politics, until Ann and David decided it was time for a change. After being offered a job at an Austin law firm in 1969, David moved the family after school let out that summer. A welcome change of pace, Austin was much more liberal politically, which fit in with the Richards' views. Also, the nightlife was exciting for the couple with its abundance of bars and live music.

Ann chose to remove herself from political life when the family first moved to Austin. She focused on her four children, the youngest of whom was beginning school.

Ann also had her hands full expanding and decorating their modest house to accommodate a family of six. Never one to lose contact with people, she still wrote to friends and hosted gatherings at her house, but did not become active in organizations beyond those like the PTA. In 1971, Ann was asked to give political advice to a woman running for state office. Although she said no at first, Ann later changed her mind and, unbeknownst to her, started down the road that would one day lead her to the governor's office.

Ann Richards: "A Woman's Place is in the Dome"

Chapter 3

GETTING INVOLVED IN POLITICS

✵✵✵✵✵

The year 1971 brought the phone call that would change the life of Ann Richards, her family, and the political landscape in Texas. A woman named Sarah Weddington wanted advice on running for the Texas legislature. Weddington made a name for herself as the lawyer who successfully argued the controversial Roe *v*. Wade case before the United State Supreme Court. Because Ann recognized the lady's name and accomplishments, she agreed to have lunch with Weddington. Ann had not planned on getting involved with politics again, but after meeting Weddington and hearing the ideas she wanted to bring to the state, Ann changed her mind and decided to run Sarah's campaign.

Sarah ran for office during a time when women were becoming more involved in politics, and she felt that she had a chance to win. Only in her mid-twenties at the time, Sarah was inexperienced in how to run a campaign, but she wanted to accomplish great things in office. An unapologetic feminist, Weddington could not find a man to help her win the office. She turned instead to women who had been politically active, which is why she asked Ann for guidance.

Some of the laws Weddington wanted to pass in the state legislature that attracted Ann to her campaign included pregnancy leave, employment equality, and reforming rape laws to protect the victim. Although Ann liked the principles Weddington was planning to base her campaign on, Richards also knew there were other issues, not involving just women, which needed to be addressed.

Ann and Sarah agreed on several topics. They took an anti-war stance against the Vietnam conflict that was being fought at the

time. In Weddington, the environmentalists found a candidate that supported their views. Sarah also promised to fight for the rights of both mothers and fathers in child custody disputes. The Weddington team found support from minorities as well.

All political campaigns cost money, and more often than not, a lot of money is needed to get a person's name recognized. One area where Sarah Weddington's campaign ran into problems was raising money. Ann helped a great deal in this area by organizing dinners and fund-raising parties at the Richards' house. Money was also provided by organizations like the Texas Women's Political Caucus. The Weddington campaign's greatest strength, however, was in the number of women volunteers that helped in everything from stuffing envelopes to passing out yard signs and bumper stickers. It was the work women traditionally did for men's campaigns, but this time the candidate was listening to the opinions of the women who volunteered their time.

Sarah Weddington's campaign for Texas legislature was about opening the door for women in politics and making people aware of women's rights issues. Sarah and Ann did not run for office thinking they were going to win easily. But in the end, Sarah did win the election. She became the representative in the legislature for Travis County, Texas, which includes the city of Austin. Sarah took office in January 1973.

The driving force behind Sarah Weddington's election, Ann Richards made it clear that, once the campaign was over, she would return to her life as mother and wife. Ann went home to spend time with her family while Sarah worked to get laws passed that helped women. In 1974, Sarah called on Ann again to help as her administrative assistant. Ann agreed and learned how the state legislature

Sarah Weddington is a graduate of McMurry College (now University) in Abilene, Texas. She earned a law degree from the University of Texas at Austin.

worked from the inside. Ann helped to create bills and followed them through the law-making process, managed the office, hired employees and interns, and learned the art of negotiation and compromise. All of the things Ann learned while working for Weddington proved valuable when the time came for Ann to run for office herself.

The Roe v. Wade ruling made abortion legal in the United States.

✳✳✳

RUNNING FOR OFFICE

David Richards was first approached to run for Travis County commissioner, but decided not to run. The Democrats, seeing an equally valuable candidate in the household, turned to Ann and asked her to run instead. Ann worried that becoming a political figure would destroy her marriage and she was not even sure if she could win the election. The office of county commissioner was seen as a man's job, since the position was in charge of building and maintaining roads and public facilities, and helping to determine tax rates. David encouraged Ann to run and even offered to take over her duties at home and with the kids. Ann decided to take a chance and put her name on the ballot.

Using many of the same fund raising tactics and volunteer help as in the Weddington campaign, Ann Richards won the election and became the first female Travis County commissioner. Because it had always been a man's job, most of the men in Ann's office were not happy about working for a woman. Trying to build a good working relationship with the men at a meeting one day, Ann asked the name of a dog she had seen hanging around her office building. One of the men replied that the dog's name was Ann Richards. The real Ann started laughing and soon the men joined in. The joke broke some of the tension in the office and everyone began working well together afterwards.

During her term as commissioner, Ann funded and established many programs. Some of the more prominent programs were for the deaf, rape victims, and families affected by Down's syndrome. She also helped establish a battered women's center.

Ann worked hard in her position as commissioner, but many of the events she attended served alcohol. Ann was no stranger to drinking. But as her political life grew her marriage began to fall apart, and she began drinking even more. She spoke to a doctor about her nightly drinking, but the doctor mistakenly told her it was nothing to worry about.

Close friends eventually talked to Ann and told her that her drinking was affecting her behavior and her relationships with people. Her friends told her she needed to get help and Ann agreed. She left for St. Mary's Hospital in Minneapolis that afternoon, even though she had fears about how this would affect her political career.

Ann stayed for four weeks and then returned to work as county commissioner. She decided not to tell people where she had been, even though the treatment at St. Mary's was successful. Ann never drank again and was a happier person for it.

Choosing not to drink anymore was not the only change in Ann Richards' life. Shortly after she returned home from seeking treatment, Ann and David separated. The couple, who had been married for almost thirty years, realized their lives had grown apart. They tried marriage counseling, but their differences could not be overcome. They divorced in 1984.

***

STATE TREASURER

While her personal life was falling apart, Ann's political career continued to rise. Having served as county commissioner and being successfully re-elected, Ann then looked to move up. The opportunity presented itself when the position of state treasurer became available. Ann's friends and colleagues encouraged her to run. Ann said she would if they could raise $200,000 in twenty-four hours for her campaign. Her network of friends and volunteers easily raised the money in the time she gave them. Ann put her name on the ballot for state treasurer.

Ann began campaigning all over the state, making stops in cities to announce that she was running for treasurer and looking for support. One of her most eager supporters was her son Dan. He helped to manage her schedule and traveled with her for the nine months of the campaign.

Not everyone got behind Ann Richards. One of Ann's former friends also decided to run for state treasurer and revealed to the press that Ann was an alcoholic who had sought treatment for the disease. The former friend made sure the media talked about her alcoholism as opposed to the issues of the campaign. Ann was honest with everyone she talked to, admitting that she was an alcoholic, had sought treatment, and did not drink anymore. Staying positive about her recovery helped Ann to eventually win the office. Ann Richards became state treasurer, the first woman to hold that office.

Appointing capable people to work under her, Ann built a staff of men and women, whites and minorities. She knew how to be a leader and give the right jobs to the right people. The treasurer is in charge of managing the people in the state treasury building and dealing with the money for the state. The people of Texas obviously thought Ann did a good job because she easily won re-election in 1986.

Ann became famous outside of Texas when asked to deliver the keynote speech at the Democratic National Convention in 1988.

Although Ann enjoyed her job as treasurer, she had to start thinking about what she wanted to do with the rest of her life. She was now in her fifties, single, and responsible for supporting herself. Ann felt that it was time for another change, an even bigger step up the ladder. Ann Richards was going to run for Governor of Texas.

Chapter 4

RUNNING FOR GOVERNOR

✳✳✳✳✳

Running for governor is more complicated than just putting your name on the ballot. First a candidate has to win the nomination of his or her chosen political party in the primary election. After a nominee becomes the candidate for either the Democratic or Republican party, he or she has to win the overall vote in a general election. This takes a great deal of time, money, and support from thousands of people.

It is not easy winning the election for the highest office in a state, but Ann Richards believed that it was time for a woman to lead Texas. In June 1988 she began telling people that she was going to run for governor. Ann officially declared herself a contender on

June 10, 1989, and the announcement was met with support from many people including her family and friends.

✳✳✳

Winning the Primary

Ann's first step would be to win the democratic primary against her ex-husband's former boss, Jim Mattox. Both candidates were popular political figures in the Democratic Party, and this made the race even closer. Both candidates were well qualified. Jim, an established attorney, also served as Texas' attorney general. Ann's political activities covered many years. She had served eight very successful years as treasurer. What made the story even more interesting is that Jim and Ann had known each other for many years. The members of the Richards family were active supporters of Jim when he ran for Congress a decade earlier.

Jim Mattox served three terms in the United States Congress, from 1977-1983.

Jim Mattox officially announced his candidacy in October 1989. The campaign for the Democratic nomination turned ugly when several candidates began smearing other applicants' reputations. Mattox dredged up Ann's history of alcohol abuse, and tossed around charges of prior drug use.

Ann wanted to run a clean race and not talk badly of her fellow candidates, but with just a few days before the election and the outcome unclear, a member of Ann's campaign team released financial information on one of the candidates. The information was so hurtful that the politician could not recover from the comments and many of his votes went instead to Ann Richards. Due to the last minute smear ads, Richards and Mattox each earned enough votes to force a runoff election. They would now be fighting to win the majority of the votes and become the Democratic Party's candidate.

The runoff was covered with less media attention because people were tired of the mudslinging. That still did not stop Mattox from continually bringing up Ann's alcoholism and alleged drug abuse. By this time, the only thing that mattered was the end result. When the votes came in, Ann Richards had won with nearly sixty percent of the votes. Relieved that the first step was done, Ann and her team prepared for the general election, the final vote to determine who would be governor.

✳✳✳

CLAYTON WILLIAMS VS. ANN RICHARDS

Ann Richards received the nomination from the Democratic Party, and Clayton Williams received the nomination from the Republican Party; these would be the two contenders for Governor of Texas in the 1990 election. Williams was a cattle and oil multimillionaire who decided to go into politics. With no previous political experience, Clayton's image and money helped him to win the Republican nomination.

Clayton's team came up with a simple, but brilliant television ad to get his name recognized. He was filmed in a white cowboy hat on his hometown ranch with men breaking rocks in the background. The commercial implied a tough-on-crime approach. With the issue of drug trafficking in the forefront of the debate, Williams' campaign supervisors thought this approach would gain votes. This commercial and generous funding (a good deal coming out of Williams' own pocket) won Williams the Republican nomination, placing him head-to-head with Ann Richards for the office of governor.

One of Williams' political ideas was to continue to play up his good ol' boy, cowboy image. As Ann was working on the runoff election against Mattox, Williams invited reporters to his ranch to watch him work rounding up cattle and riding on horseback. While none could dispute that he was a cowboy, some did question his ability to lead the state.

With the runoff election complete, Ann now had to look at her strategy for the general election. Voters did not like the mudslinging of the primaries, and Ann's election funds were seriously depleted, especially compared to Williams'. Raising money was easier after Richards won the primary, but overcoming the negative media attention she received would prove more difficult. Up to this point, Williams was seen as a man with a flawless public image; but that would not last for long.

One of Clayton Williams' missteps was in refusing to debate Ann Richards at the beginning of the campaign. Voters saw this as cowardly. Also, at a gathering to talk

Clayton W. Williams, Jr. was born in 1931 in Alpine, Texas. His nickname was "Claytie."

Miriam "Ma" Ferguson was the first female governor of Texas, elected in 1924 and again in 1932, Ann Richards became the second woman governor in 1990.

to the Greater Dallas Crime Commissions. Richards approached Williams to shake hands, but he refused. Many people saw this as very ungentlemanly and Richards gained more voter support after the incident. Williams also admitted to the press, shortly before Election Day, that he had not paid taxes in 1986. This was very harmful to his campaign. Richards, who had released all of her income tax records, scolded Williams for using loopholes to avoid paying taxes when the people he was fighting to represent worked hard and had to pay their taxes. Each of these mistakes earned Ann Richards more support, and lessened the popularity of Clayton Williams. By Election Day the candidates were about even, and no one knew who was going to win.

✳✳✳

A Woman's Place is in the Dome

Across the state, polls opened on the morning of November 6, 1990. Beautiful weather meant high voter turnout. Ann Richards spent the day with friends and family, even playing bridge for a few hours in the afternoon. Results came in throughout the day, first showing Ann in the lead and then Clayton. Finally around 8:30 in the evening, the press projected that Ann had won the election. The amount of votes separating Richards and Williams was less than 100,000 out of the nearly 4 million. The narrow margin did not matter—Ann Richards was the next Governor of Texas!

Ann walked into the ballroom of the Hyatt Regency amid the deafening shouts of her loyal followers. Without saying a word, Ann raised a T-shirt with the encouraging words, "A Woman's Place Is In The Dome." The Dome is the capitol building in Austin. This con-

The election of 1990 was the 45th election for the governor's office in the State of Texas.

firmed to all of Ann's supporters and the state, that Ann was indeed the victor that evening, and Texas would have a woman governor for the second time in its history.

Ann eventually calmed the crowd long enough to thank everyone for their efforts in getting her elected. In speaking to the people gathered, she told them, "We're going to join hands and march up Congress Avenue and we're going to take back the capitol for the people of Texas!" The crowd was so caught up in the excitement of the evening they began crowding Ann Richards to the point that she had to withdraw to a suite upstairs. Tired and overjoyed, Ann went to sleep that night knowing she had an important job to do—taking care of the people of Texas.

Chapter 5

ACCOMPLISHMENTS AS GOVERNOR

✳✳✳✳✳

Governor Ann Richards' term in office brought great improvements and success to the State of Texas. Keeping her promise from the night she won the election on January 15, 1991, Ann and a crowd of supporters and well-wishers gathered in Austin. They marched the twelve blocks to the capitol where Ann Richards was sworn into office.

The rest of the day and into the early hours of the next morning, celebrations were held in honor of the new governor. The first celebration, a fried chicken picnic, was held on the grounds of the capitol. For only five dollars, anyone could come. Even the social events that evening, which were normally a costly affair, averaged only thirty dollars a ticket.

Not only were the celebrations varied in the type of people who attended, Ann's new appointments after taking office were also very diverse. In total, about 400 positions were needed for state boards and commissions. Ann filled them with competent people, many of whom were women and minorities. In fact, Ann appointed more women and minorities to positions in the state government than any previous administration. That is not to say that there were no problems at all with the people she appointed.

In one instance it was discovered that Lena Guerrero, Ann's selection for the Railroad Commission, had misrepresented herself when saying she earned a degree with honors from the University of Texas. It was later discovered that Guerrero had not even graduated. Regardless of the occasional mistakes, the vast majority of appointees were highly qualified and successful.

Governor Richards, wanting to reform the tarnished reputation of

Texas politics, hired Barbara Jordan as her special advisor on ethical standards. Jordan was picked because she had served on the United States House of Representatives' Judiciary Committee and had voted to impeach President Richard Nixon. Ann's success in ethics reform included a law requiring lobbyists to report how much money was spent on politicians and a law saying lobbyists could be punished for bribing public officials.

During her term in office, Richards supported another successful and widely acclaimed program aimed at increasing funding for Texas schools. The state lottery became very popular and Governor Richards bought the first ticket on May 29, 1992.

Not all of her attempts to improve school finance were as well received. Ann supported the "Robin Hood Plan," a law which moved money from wealthier school districts to poorer districts in an attempt to even out school funding. This way of taxing property was not very popular. Eventually, the plan was ruled uncon-

stitutional in Texas and eliminated.

Some of the other improvements Governor Richards

made to the State of Texas dealt with changing the state

prison system. A drug abuse program was started to keep

inmates sober while in prison and after they were

released. The number of violent convicts released was

decreased, while prison space was increased, to help solve

the problem of a growing prison population in Texas.

While the nation's economy struggled in the early

1990s, Ann took steps to improve the economy of Texas.

During her tenure as governor, the number of businesses

that relocated to Texas was the highest in the nation. In

1991, a time when the economy for the rest of the United

States shrank, the efforts of Ann Richards helped the Texas

The Texas State Capitol building is taller than the U.S. Capitol Building.

economy grow by 2%. Not only did new companies move to Texas, Ann also kept companies operating in the state. She convinced General Motors to keep its Arlington plant running and the people that worked there employed. Ann also boosted the economy by encouraging people to see Texas as a tourist destination. The entertainment industry expanded in Texas after Ann traveled to Los Angeles and promoted the attributes of the Lone Star State. By the end of her service as governor, a half-a-million more Texans were employed than when she first took office.

While Ann Richards was a very popular personality, she did veto two pieces of legislation that some critics say may have cost her re-election. One bill would have caused the destruction of the Edwards Aquifer, an underground water system that serves south central Texas,

Barbara Jordan was the first African-American woman to deliver the keynote address at the Democratic National Convention.

including the city of San Antonio. The aquifer is also home to several endangered species. Ann decided the environment and the aquifer should be preserved and she vetoed the bill. The other piece of legislation was a bill that would allow the people of Texas to carry concealed handguns, automatic weapons, and "cop-killer bullets." Ann said she would not allow that to happen during her time in public office. She was very proud of having vetoed that bill. Her successor signed the concealed weapons bill into law.

✳✳✳

After Leaving Office

Although Ann Richards remained very popular throughout her tenure as governor, she was not re-elected in 1994. The nation as a whole seemed to be caught up

According to the Texas Parks and Wildlife, there are currently 28 types of threatened or endangered mammals in Texas.

in a movement for change. Many politicians already in office were voted out in favor of a new viewpoint; Ann was one of these. Her opponent, George W. Bush, defeated Ann in the next election. Only a few years later, Bush became President of the United States.

Ann decided to play a more behind-the-scenes role after leaving office. She worked as an advisor for a public strategies company and a law firm. She was remembered on the national political stage for her popular 1988 Democratic keynote speech, where she issued the famous line about then vice president George H.W. Bush, "Poor George, he can't help it. . . . He was born with a silver foot in his mouth." Because she remained such a well-known Democratic figure, Ann also remained active in politics by campaigning for Democratic candidates during the presidential elections. There was even some talk of Ann running for president, but she quickly squashed that idea.

Ann Richards supported the arts and entertainment industry and in return, it was fond of her. She narrated a documentary titled *Barbecue: A Texas Love Story*. In a fun guest spot, Ann Richards voiced an animated version of herself in the 2004 Disney film *Home on the Range*. It wasn't her first time lending her talents to film. During her time as governor, Ann also voiced her character on an episode of the television series, "King of the Hill."

In 2006, plans were announced for "The Ann Richards School for Young Women Leaders" in Austin, Texas. It is a college preparatory school for girls in grades 6-12. The intent of the school is to focus on math, science, and technology. Also announced in 2006, Ann Richards revealed that she had been diagnosed with cancer.

In 1989, George W. Bush became one of the owners of the Texas Rangers, a major league baseball team.

The life of Ann Richards is a testament to strength of character, hard work, and overcoming obstacles. She worked just as hard being a wife and mother as she did serving the people of Texas. She overcame her addiction to alcohol and became an inspiration to many. She was the second female governor of Texas and faithfully served the citizens of the state. She is remembered as a voice for women and minorities, a leader who can be admired, a visionary for the future of Texas, and a friend to all. Texas and the nation felt the loss of a great person when Ann Richards died of throat cancer on September 13, 2006. Her lasting impact on the people and politics of Texas will never be forgotten.

Timeline

1933—Dorothy Ann Willis is born in Lakeview, Texas

1944—Ann and her mother move to San Diego where Ann's father is stationed with the Navy

1945—Ann and her family move back to Lakeview, Texas, after the end of World War II

1950—Ann graduates from Waco High School

1953—Ann and David Richards are married

1954—Ann graduates from Baylor University; Ann receives teaching certificate from the University of Texas at Austin

1957—Daughter Lynn Cecile Richards is born

1959—Son Dan Richards is born

1962—Son Clark Richards is born

1964—Daughter Ellen Richards is born

1969—The Richards family moves to Austin

1971—Ann manages Sarah Weddington's campaign for a seat in the Texas Legislature

1976—Ann is elected Travis County Commissioner

1982—Ann is elected Texas State Treasurer

1984—Ann checks herself into an alcohol rehabilitation program; David and Ann are divorced

1990—Ann Richards is elected Governor of Texas

1994—Ann loses the race for re-election to George W. Bush

2006—September 13, Ann dies from esophageal (throat) cancer

Glossary

Alcoholism—repeated, compulsive consumption use of alcoholic drinks

Campaign—a competition by rival political candidates for public office

Debate—a formal contest in which the affirmative and negative sides of an idea are supported by opposing speakers

Draft—selecting one or more people from the general public for mandatory military service

Ethics—the code of behavior leading an individual or a group

Governor—the person in charge of a state government

Integration—the action of incorporating a racial group into a community

Legislature—persons who make or change or get rid of laws

Parliamentarian—a person who knows the formal rules and procedures of meetings

Primary—a preliminary election in which voters of each party nominate candidates for office

Segregation—the practice of separating people of different races, classes, or ethnic groups, as in schools, and housing, especially as a form of discrimination

Treasurer—an officer of a government, in charge of receiving and payment of money

United States Supreme Court—the highest federal court in the United States; has final authority in all legal decisions and over all other courts in the nation

Veto—the right of a president, governor, or other chief executive to disallow bills passed by the legislature

Further Reading

Dorothy Schainman Siegel. *Ann Richards: Politician, Feminist, Survivor*. Springfield, N.J.: Enslow Publishers, Inc., 1996.

Richard Sobol. *Governor: In the Company of Ann W. Richards Governor of Texas*. Dutton, N.Y.: Cobblehill Books, 1994.

Mike Shropshire and Frank Schaefer. *The Thorny Rose of Texas: An Intimate Portrait of Governor Ann Richards*. New York, N.Y.: Carol Publishing Group, 1994.

Sue Tolleson-Rinehart and Jeanie R. Stanley. *Claytie and the Lady: Ann Richards, Gender, and Politics in Texas*. Austin, Tex.: University of Texas Press, 1994.

Celia Morris. *Storming the Statehouse: Running for Governor with Ann Richards and Dianne Feinstein*. New York, N.Y.: Charles Scribner's Sons, 1992.

Ann Richards with Peter Knobler. *Straight from the Heart: My Life in Politics and Other Places*. New York, N.Y.: Simon and Schuster, 1989.

WEBSITES

http://www.tshaonline.org/handbook/online/articles/RR/fri62.html
(biography of Ann Richards and her political accomplishments)

http://en.wikipedia.org/wiki/Ann_Richards (biographical sketch of
Ann Richards life and political career, with picture)

http://www.tsl.state.tx.us/governors/modern/page3.html#Richards
(a short description of Ann Richards political career, with links to
several images of Richards, including the one of her on a motorcycle.)

http://www.quotationspage.com/quotes/Ann_Richards/ (famous
quotes by Richards)

http://www.americanrhetoric.com/speeches/annrichards1988dnc.htm
(a copy of the speech Ann Richards gave at the Democratic
National Convention in 1988)

INDEX